THE TAILOR OF GLOSTER

MRS TITTLE-MOUSE

SQUIRREL NUTKIN

NUTS

TOM KITTEN

PETER RABBIT

A FARMYARD TALE FOR RALPH AND BETSY

*Frederick Warne has a continuing commitment to reproduce Beatrix
Potter's exquisite watercolours to the highest possible standard. In 1993 and 1994,
taking advantage of the latest advances in printing technology and expertise, entirely new film
was made from her original book illustrations. The drawings are now reproduced with a quality
and a degree of authenticity never before attainable in print.*

FREDERICK WARNE

Published by the Penguin Group
27 Wrights Lane, London W8 5TZ, England
Penguin Books USA Inc., 375 Hudson Street, New York, N.Y. 10014, USA
Penguin Books Australia Ltd, Ringwood, Victoria, Australia
Penguin Books Canada Ltd, 10 Alcorn Avenue, Toronto, Ontario, Canada M4V 3B2
Penguin Books (N.Z.) Ltd, 182-190 Wairau Road, Auckland 10, New Zealand

Penguin Books Ltd, Registered Offices: Harmondsworth, Middlesex, England

First published 1908 by Frederick Warne
This edition with new reproductions of Beatrix Potter's book illustrations first published 1997

Colour reproduction by
Saxon Photolitho Ltd, Norwich
Printed and bound in Great Britain by
William Clowes Limited, Beccles and London

THE TALE OF
JEMIMA PUDDLE-DUCK

❋

BY BEATRIX POTTER

FREDERICK WARNE

WHAT a funny sight it is to see a brood of ducklings with a hen!

—Listen to the story of Jemima Puddle-duck, who was annoyed because the farmer's wife would not let her hatch her own eggs.

HER sister-in-law, Mrs. Rebeccah
Puddle-duck, was perfectly willing to leave
the hatching to some one else—"I have not
the patience to
sit on a nest
for twenty-
eight days;
and no more
have you,
Jemima. You
would let
them go cold;
you know you
would!"

"I wish to
hatch my own
eggs; I will hatch them all by myself,"
quacked Jemima Puddle-duck.

SHE tried to hide her eggs; but they were always found and carried off.

Jemima Puddle-duck became quite desperate. She determined to make a nest right away from the farm.

SHE set off on a fine spring afternoon along the cart-road that leads over the hill.

She was wearing a shawl and a poke bonnet.

WHEN she reached the top of the hill, she saw a wood in the distance.

She thought that it looked a safe quiet spot.

JEMIMA PUDDLE-DUCK was not much in the habit of flying. She ran downhill a few yards flapping her shawl, and then she jumped off into the air.

She flew beautifully when she had got a good start.

She skimmed along over the tree-tops until she saw an open place in the middle of the wood, where the trees and brushwood had been cleared.

JEMIMA alighted rather heavily, and began to waddle about in search of a convenient dry nesting-place. She rather fancied a tree-stump amongst some tall fox-gloves.

But—seated upon the stump, she was startled to find an elegantly dressed gentleman reading a newspaper.

He had black prick ears and sandy coloured whiskers.

"Quack?" said Jemima Puddle-duck, with her head and her bonnet on one side— "Quack?"

The gentleman raised his eyes above his newspaper and looked curiously at Jemima—

"Madam, have you lost your way?" said he. He had a long bushy tail which he was sitting upon, as the stump was somewhat damp.

JEMIMA thought him mighty civil and handsome. She explained that she had not lost her way, but that she was trying to find a convenient dry nesting-place.

"AH! is that so? indeed!" said the gentleman with sandy whiskers, looking curiously at Jemima. He folded up the newspaper, and put it in his coat-tail pocket.

Jemima complained of the superfluous hen.

"Indeed! how interesting! I wish I could meet with that fowl. I would teach it to mind its own business!

"But as to a nest—there is no difficulty: I have a sackful of feathers in my wood-shed.

"NO, my dear madam, you will be in
nobody's way. You may sit there as long as you
like," said the bushy long-tailed gentleman.

He led the way to a very retired,
dismal-looking house amongst the fox-gloves.

It was built
of faggots
and turf,
and there
were two
broken
pails, one on
top of
another, by
way of a
chimney.

"THIS is my summer residence; you would not find my earth—my winter house—so convenient," said the hospitable gentleman.

There was a tumble-down shed at the back of the house, made of old soap-boxes. The gentleman opened the door, and showed Jemima in.

THE shed was almost quite full of feathers—
it was almost suffocating; but it was
comfortable and very soft.

Jemima Puddle-duck was rather surprised to
find such a vast quantity of feathers. But it
was very comfortable; and she made a nest
without any trouble at all.

WHEN she came out, the sandy whiskered gentleman was sitting on a log reading the newspaper—at least he had it spread out, but he was looking over the top of it.

He was so polite, that he seemed almost sorry to let Jemima go home for the night. He promised to take great care of her nest until she came back again next day.

He said he loved eggs and ducklings; he should be proud to see a fine nestful in his wood-shed.

JEMIMA PUDDLE-DUCK
came every
afternoon; she laid
nine eggs in the
nest. They
were greeny
white and very
large. The foxy
gentleman
admired them

immensely. He used to turn them over and
count them when Jemima was not there.

At last Jemima told him that she intended to
begin to sit next day—"and I will bring a bag
of corn with me, so that I need never leave
my nest until the eggs are hatched. They
might catch cold," said the conscientious
Jemima.

"MADAM, I beg you not to trouble yourself with a bag; I will provide oats. But before you commence your tedious sitting, I intend to give you a treat. Let us have a dinner-party all to ourselves!

"May I ask you to bring up some herbs from the farm-garden to make a savoury omelette? Sage and thyme, and mint and two onions, and some parsley. I will provide lard for the stuff—lard for the omelette," said the hospitable gentleman with sandy whiskers.

Jemima Puddle-duck was a simpleton: not even the mention of sage and onions made her suspicious.

She went round the farm-garden, nibbling off snippets of all the different sorts of herbs that are used for stuffing roast duck.

AND she waddled into the kitchen, and got two onions out of a basket.

The collie-dog Kep met her coming out. "What are you doing with those onions? Where do you go every afternoon by yourself, Jemima Puddle-duck?"

Jemima was rather in awe of the collie; she told him the whole story.

The collie listened, with his wise head on one side; he grinned when she described the polite gentleman with sandy whiskers.

HE asked several questions about the wood,
and about the exact position of the house and
shed.

Then he went out, and trotted down the
village. He went to look for two fox-hound
puppies who were out at walk with the
butcher.

JEMIMA PUDDLE-DUCK went up the cart-road for the last time, on a sunny afternoon. She was rather burdened with bunches of herbs and two onions in a bag.

She flew over the wood, and alighted opposite the house of the bushy long-tailed gentleman.

HE was sitting on a log; he sniffed the air, and kept glancing uneasily round the wood. When Jemima alighted he quite jumped.

"Come into the house as soon as you have looked at your eggs. Give me the herbs for the omelette. Be sharp!"

He was rather abrupt. Jemima Puddle-duck had never heard him speak like that.

She felt surprised, and uncomfortable.

WHILE she was inside she heard pattering
feet round the back of the shed. Some one
with a black nose sniffed at the bottom of the
door, and then locked it.

Jemima became much alarmed.

A MOMENT afterwards there were most awful noises—barking, baying, growls and howls, squealing and groans.

And nothing more was ever seen of that foxy-whiskered gentleman.

PRESENTLY Kep opened the door of the shed, and let out Jemima Puddle-duck.

Unfortunately the puppies rushed in and gobbled up all the eggs before he could stop them.

He had a bite on his ear and both the puppies were limping.

Jemima Puddle-duck was escorted home in tears on account of those eggs.

SHE laid some more in June, and she was
permitted to keep them herself: but only four
of them hatched.

Jemima Puddle-duck said that it was
because of her nerves; but she had always
been a bad sitter.